BOYS RULE!

Gone Fishing

Felice Arena and Phil Kettle

illustrated by
Susy Boyer

RISING ★ STARS

s/3078723

First published in Great Britain by
RISING STARS UK LTD 2004
76 Farnaby Road, Bromley, BR1 4BH

Reprinted 2004

For information visit our website at:
www.risingstars-uk.com

British Library Cataloguing in Publication Data

A CIP record for this book is available from the British Library.

ISBN: 1-904591-68-X

First published in 2003 by
MACMILLAN EDUCATION AUSTRALIA PTY LTD
627 Chapel Street, South Yarra, Australia 3141

Associated companies and representatives throughout the world.

Project Management by Limelight Press Pty Ltd
Cover and text design by Lore Foye
Illustrations by Susy Boyer

Printed and bound in Great Britain by
Mackays of Chatham plc, Chatham, Kent

BOYS RULE!

Contents

Tom   Joey

CHAPTER 1

Before Catching the Big One

Best friends Joey and Tom have gone fishing with Joey's father to a river not too far from where they live.

While Joey's dad finds the perfect spot to cast out his line, Joey and Tom wander off and pick a good spot for themselves. Joey tries to place a worm on a hook while Tom looks closely over his shoulder—it is his first time fishing.

Tom "Do you think a worm
feels pain?"

Joey "No."

Tom "But it's wriggling a lot."

Joey "Yeah that's what a worm
does, especially when it has a hook
stuck in it."

Tom "So then it is in pain."

Joey "No it's not. It's a worm. It doesn't feel anything."

Tom "What about if we use bread as bait? I could use bits of the sandwich Mum made me."

Joey "No way! Fish like worms. That's what they eat."

Tom "Well, I might still use bread anyway."

Joey "It doesn't hurt them—really. Cross my heart and hope to die, stick a needle in my eye!"

Tom "What about a *hook* in your eye?"

Joey "Yeah, good one! Just look at it. It's not in pain."

Joey raises the worm on the hook only centimetres away from Tom's face. He then suddenly screams out, "RAH!!!". Tom jumps back startled, falling over onto the tackle box. Joey laughs.

Joey "Gotcha!"

Tom "Really funny. I'm still goin' to use bread."

Joey "Then you're not goin' to catch anything. Here, give me your hook. I'll put a worm on for you—scaredy cat!"

Tom "I'm not scared."

Joey "Yes you are. Just like a girl—
like my sister Sarah. She freaks
out over everything. Even ants."

Tom "No way! I'm not like that. Give
me a worm then. I'll show you."

CHAPTER 2

Waiting for the Big One

Tom puts a worm onto a hook even though he almost feels like throwing up while doing it. Joey is ready to cast his fishing line.

Joey "Okay, fishies here we come! Stand back Tom, I don't want to hook you or you'll end up like Mrs. Hurley."

Tom "Mrs. Hurley, our teacher Mrs. Hurley?"

Joey "Yeah. Why do you think she's got a pierced nose?"

Tom "Because she's really trendy and cool?"

Joey "Nope! 'Cos she got a fishhook caught in it. One of the Year Six boys told me."

Tom "No way!"

Joey "Yes! She went fishing with her boyfriend once and stood too close to him while he was throwing in his line. The hook got stuck right in the side of her left nostril.

"When her boyfriend got it out, the hole was so big that she decided to get a diamond stud in it to cover it up. So, you'd better stand back, unless you think you'd look good with a pierced nose."

Joey throws his line in and Tom does the same. Both boys just sit and wait.

Joey "I think I've got a bite."

Tom "Really? That's quick!"

Joey "Shhh! You'll scare it away."

Tom (whispering) "Do you think it's a fish?"

Joey "No, it's a crocodile."

Tom (whispering) "Really?"

Joey "No! Of course it's a fish! But I think it's gone now."

Tom "You know I got my highest score last night on 'Beetle Raider 3000'—I got 52 022 points."

Joey "Cool! Is that Level Six?"

Tom "Yes."

Joey "I can only make it to Level
Five. Tom look! Quick! You've got a
bite and it's a big one."

CHAPTER 3

Catching the Big One
(almost)

Joey and Tom struggle to reel in a
large fish that has hooked itself onto
Tom's line. Suddenly the line goes
loose. The fish has got away.

Joey "Oh man! Did you see that! It was humungous."

Tom "Unreal! It felt like it weighed a ton."

Joey "That's for sure! I can't believe it got away. I bet it was the biggest fish in this river."

Tom "How big do you think it was?"

Joey "At least as big as us, even bigger. It would've been a world record in fishing."

Tom "Awwh cool! I would've been famous. I would've been interviewed on television and everything."

Joey "What do you mean *you* would've been famous? We *both* would've been famous."

Tom "Yeah, but it was my line."

Joey "So? It was my fishing rod. I'm goin' to tell Dad that we almost caught a big one. Just wait here and look after my line. It might come back again."

Joey runs over to his dad, then returns to Tom.

Tom "Has your dad caught any?"

Joey "No. He just said he's enjoying the serenity."

Tom "What's serenity?"

Joey "It sort of means peaceful, I think."

Tom "You mean like being bored?"

Joey "Yeah, sort of. Are you bored?"

Tom "Yeah, a bit. And hungry!"

Joey "Then have that sandwich your mum made."

Tom "I can't. I just gave it to a whole bunch of fish."

Joey "*What*!?"

CHAPTER 4

Forgetting the Big One

Joey suddenly looks down at the water and is amazed to see a large school of fish swimming near the surface, gulping and nipping at the sandwich Tom has just thrown in.

Joey "Brilliant idea Tom! Look at them all! I'm goin' to try to catch one."

Tom "Me too!"

Both boys scramble for their fishing rods, scaring the fish away in the process. Disappointed yet again, they sit down and wait for them to reappear.

Joey "That was amazing. There must've been twenty of them."

Tom "Yeah. I wish they'd come back. It'd be a shame to waste what's left of the sandwich."

Joey and Tom wait patiently without saying a word to each other, for what seems a very, very, long minute.

Joey "Have you played the new
Gameboy game called 'Fishnet'?"

Tom "No. Is it any good?"

Joey "Yeah, it's awesome. You have
to net as many fish as you can in a
set time to get to the next level. It's
in the car. Do you want to play?"

Tom "Yeah, let's go!"

Joey and Tom make their way back to Joey's dad's car. Joey's father calls out to them. "What about the fishing?"

Joey and Tom (chuckling) "That's what we're goin' to do."

A few minutes later Joey's father joins Tom and Joey in the car, ready to take them home.

"So, Tom, what did you learn from your first time fishing?" he asks before driving off.

Tom looks up, while Joey
continues to play his Gameboy.

Tom "Um ... fish really do like
bread, and bring a Gameboy just
in case you feel a bit of serenity
creeping in."

Tom

Fishing Lingo

Joey

bait What you put on your hook so that you might catch a fish.

fishing rod What you use to catch a fish. The bait goes on the end of it.

fresh water Water that hasn't got salt in it. Most rivers are fresh water.

sinker A small metal ball you tie onto your fishing line to keep the line under the water.

snag When you get your line caught on something under the water.

BOYS RULE!

Fishing Must-dos

☞ Make sure you have bait on the hook before you cast your line into the water. If you don't want to catch a fish, don't put any bait on your hook!

☞ If you are looking for worms to use as bait, look in the garden. But when you are digging, make sure that you don't dig up any plants.

☞ Make sure that you throw back any undersized fish that you catch.

☞ Only keep as many fish as you think you can eat.

☞ When you cast your line, don't cast too close to trees or you might get your line tangled in the branches.

☞ To catch freshwater fish, you should fish in rivers, lakes or ponds.

☞ If you go fly-fishing, you don't have to put live flies on your hook. The flies for fly-fishing are handmade.

☞ If you are fishing from a boat, make sure that you wear a life jacket.

☞ Remember to take some money with you when you go fishing. You might need the money to buy some fish at the fish shop on the way home.

☞ When you find a really good fishing spot, make sure you don't tell anyone. You don't want all the good fish caught before you go back there!

BOYS RULE!
Fishing
Instant Info

The most ferocious freshwater fish is the South American piranha. It has razor-sharp teeth. The piranha loves blood and the taste of flesh. In 1981 more than 300 people were killed and eaten by piranha when their boat sunk in Brazil.

The biggest man-eating fish is the great white shark. The average length of a great white shark is 4.3 to 4.6 metres.

The largest mouth in the world belongs to the bowhead whale— 5 metres long and 4 metres wide. Its tongue weighs 900 kilograms.

The longest animal in the sea is a type of jellyfish. Some can be as long as 50 metres.

The largest sea-living mammal is the blue whale. Its average length is a massive 35 metres. Some blue whales have weighed as much as 190 tons!

The least experienced fisher-kid always seems to catch the most fish.

The worse your line tangles, the more fish seem to have been caught by everyone else.

Fishing will do a lot for you but the one thing it won't do is make you truthful!

Think Tank

1 What are worms good for when you go fishing?

2 Where do you catch freshwater fish?

3 What is a snag?

4 What do you do with undersized fish?

5 What is the biggest man-eating fish in the world?

6 Are crabs fish?

7 What do you use a sinker for?

8 What should you wear when you are in a boat?

Answers

8 You should always wear a life jacket when in a boat.

7 A sinker keeps your line at the bottom of the river or the ocean.

6 No, crabs are not fish. They are crustaceans.

5 The great white shark is the biggest man-eating fish in the world.

4 You kiss undersized fish then throw them back.

3 A snag is what you get when you get your line caught on something.

2 You won't catch freshwater fish in the ocean. You catch them in a river, pond or lake.

1 Worms are good for bait—you just have to learn how to put them on your hook.

How did you score?

- If you got 8 correct answers, you might be good enough to catch a shark!

- If you got 4 correct answers then maybe you need to get some fishing lessons.

- If you got fewer than 2 correct answers you'd better get your fish from a fish shop.

Felice → ← Phil

Hi Guys!

We have loads of fun reading and want you to, too. We both believe that being a good reader is really important and so cool.

Try out our suggestions to help you have fun as you read.

At school, why don't you use "Gone Fishing" as a play and you and your friends can be the actors. Set the scene for your play. Try not to get the line caught in anyone's hair. Maybe you can use your imagination to pretend that you are about to catch the biggest fish ever.

So ... have you decided who is going to be Joey and who is going to be Tom? Now, with your friends, read and act out our story in front of the class.

We have a lot of fun when we go to schools and read our stories. After we finish the kids all clap really loudly. When you've finished your play your classmates will do the same. Just remember to look out of the window— there might be a talent scout from a television station watching you!

Reading at home is really important and a lot of fun as well.

Take our books home and get someone in your family to read them with you. Maybe they can take on a part in the story.

Remember, reading is a whole lot of fun.

So, as the frog in the local pond would say, Read-it!

And remember, Boys Rule!

BOYS RULE!
When We Were Kids

Felice *Phil*

Felice "What's the biggest fish you ever caught?"

Phil "I once caught a fish in the Murray River that was so big it needed a tow truck to take it out of the river."

Felice "So what did you do with it?"

Phil "I threw it back because it smiled at me and I felt sorry for it."

Felice "Was anyone there to see this giant fish?"

Phil "No, I was by myself."

Felice "Sounds fishy to me!"

What a Laugh!

Q What do you call a man who likes fishing?

A Rod.

43

BOYS RULE!

Read about the fun that boys have in these **BOYS RULE!** titles:

Gone Fishing

The Tree House

Golf Legend

Camping Out

Bike Daredevils

Water Rats

Skateboard Dudes

Tennis Ace

Basketball Buddies

Secret Agent Heroes

Wet World

Rock Star

and more ... !

44